E   Nidey, Kelli
Nid   When Autumn Falls
           20.96

1/5/07

When Autumn Falls

Kelli Nidey

ILLUSTRATIONS BY

Susan Swan

ALBERT WHITMAN & COMPANY, MORTON GROVE, ILLINOIS

With love to my sons, Mitch and Weston, and
in memory of Avis.—K.N.

For Celeste, the bionic grandma, and Richard,
Superbrother, with powers far beyond
those of ordinary mortals.—S.S.

Library of Congress Cataloging-in-Publication Data

Nidey, Kelli.
When autumn falls / by Kelli Nidey ; illustrated by Susan Swan.
p. cm.
Summary: Observes the aptly named fall season,
characterized by falling leaves, falling apples, falling players on the
football field, and falling temperatures.
ISBN 10: 0-8075-0490-4 (hardcover) ISBN 13: 978-0-8075-0490-1 (hardcover)
ISBN 10: 0-8075-0491-2 (paperback) ISBN 13: 978-0-8075-0491-8 (paperback)
(1. Autumn—Fiction.) I. Swan, Susan, 1944- ill. II. Title.
PZ7.N5615Wh 2004 (E)—dc22 2004001689

The design is by Susan Swan and Carol Gildar.

For more information about Albert Whitman & Company,
visit our web site at www.albertwhitman.com.

Leaves
on the
trees fall—

red,
gold,
yellow,
brown,
and
orange
come
down.

The temperature falls,
bringing cooler weather.
Grab your jacket or your sweater.

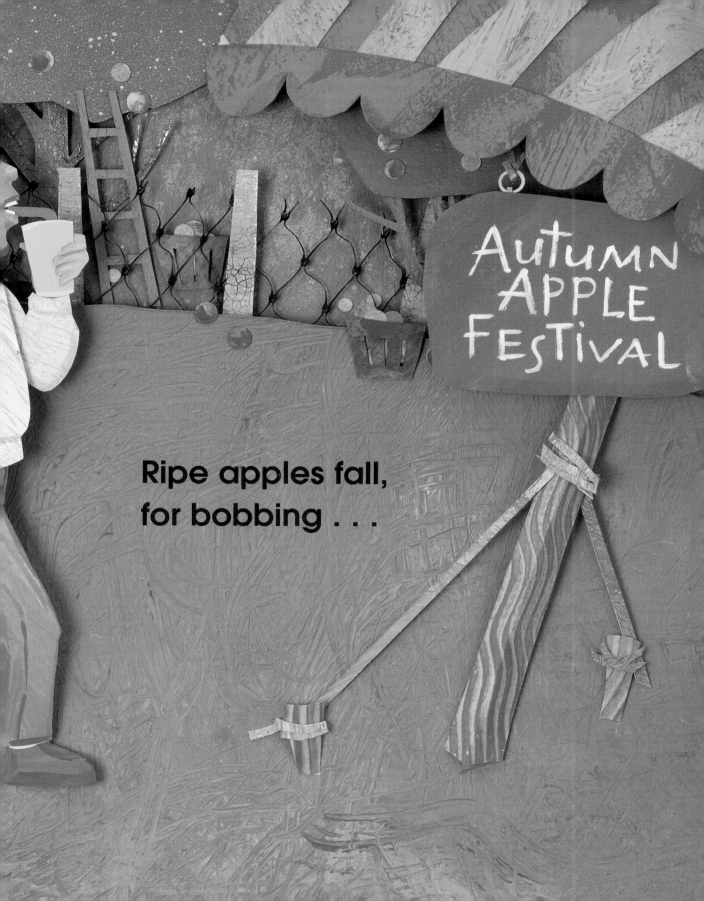

Ripe apples fall,
for bobbing . . .

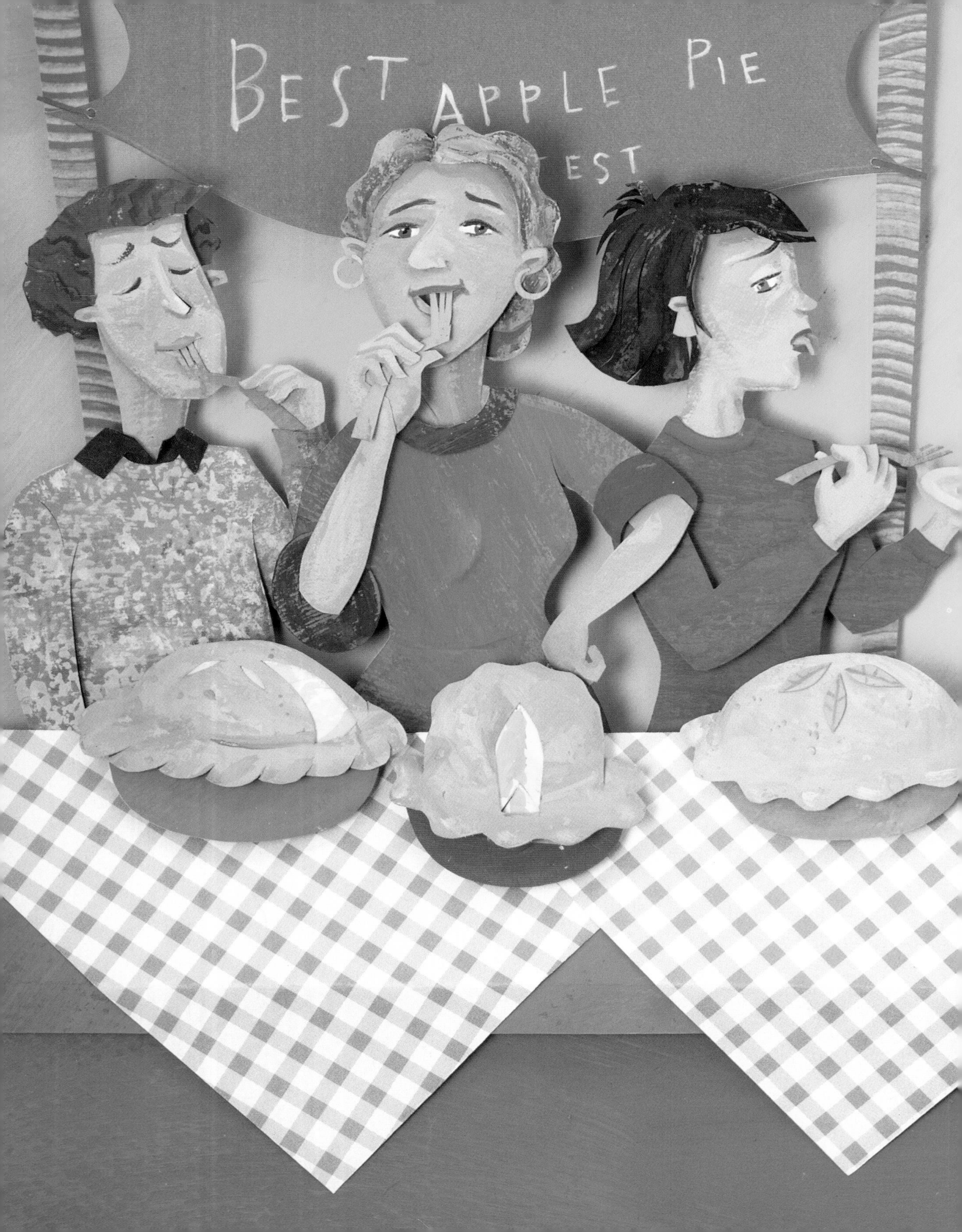
BEST APPLE PIE

and baking,
and caramel apple making.

Seeds fall from the last sunflowers,
and pumpkins come loose
from the vines.

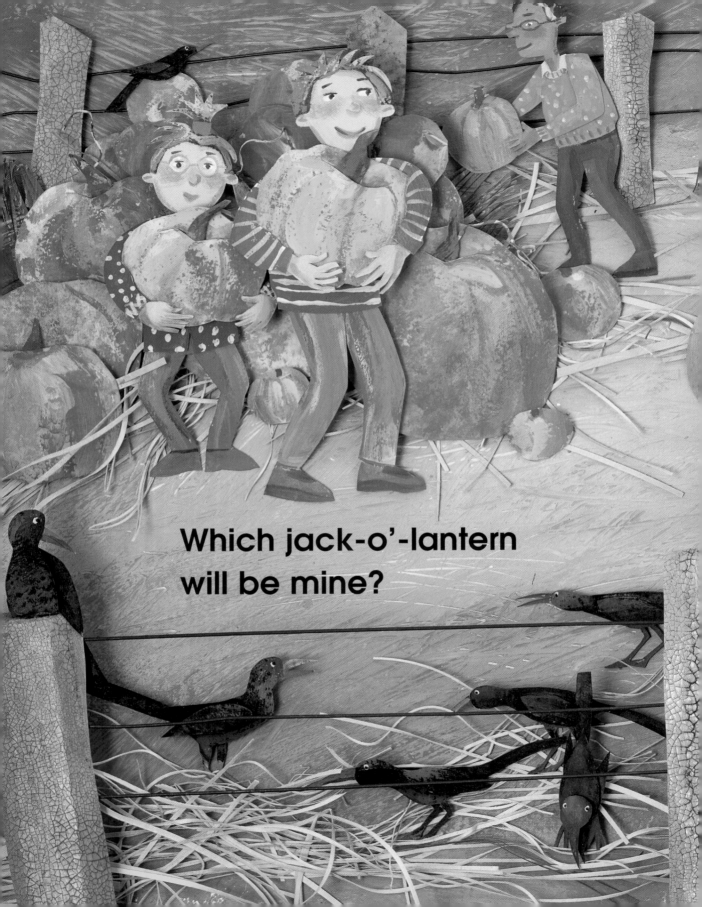

Which jack-o'-lantern
will be mine?

Football players fall
into the end zone—
whose hand is on the ball?

Little children fall
into piles of leaves
stacked high.

As friends walk by,
footsteps fall
on the crunched-up leaves.

Sunlight falls
through
the almost-bare trees.

And then the raindrops fall,
washing the last leaves away.

Evening falls
earlier in the day . . .

as the days fall
shorter.

We call it *fall.*